April Adventure

Brian sat up and rubbed his eyes. "Hey, what's this?" he asked. He held up a blue plastic egg. "It was on my pillow!"

"I found one, too," Bradley said, showing his egg. "My egg had a note inside."

Brian yanked his egg apart. A folded paper fell out. "Mine does, too!" he said.

Nate and Lucy soon found plastic eggs in their sleeping bags.

"We all have notes!" Lucy said. "Mine says, GO WHERE A ROSE GROWS. SIGNED, THE SHADOW."

"Mine says, GET DRESSED," Brian said.

Nate crawled out of his sleeping bag. "Mine says, THERE YOU WILL FIND DIRECTIONS TO THE TREASURE. It's signed THE SHADOW, too."

"Cool, it's a treasure hunt!" Lucy said. "I love treasure hunts! But who's the Shadow?"

Calendar Mysteries
April Adventure

by Ron Roy

illustrated by
John Steven Gurney

A STEPPING STONE BOOK™

Random House New York

This book is dedicated to Judy Taylor.
—R.R.

To Central Elementary School in Sidney, Ohio
—J.S.G.

Text copyright © 2010 by Ron Roy
Illustrations and map copyright © 2010 by John Steven Gurney

All rights reserved.
Published in the United States by Random House Children's Books,
a division of Random House, Inc., New York.

Random House and the colophon are registered trademarks and A Stepping Stone Book and the colophon are trademarks of Random House, Inc.

Visit us on the Web!
www.ronroy.com
www.randomhouse.com/kids

Educators and librarians, for a variety of teaching tools, visit us at
www.randomhouse.com/teachers

Library of Congress Cataloging-in-Publication Data
Roy, Ron.
April adventure / by Ron Roy ; illustrated by John Steven Gurney. — 1st ed.
     p.   cm. — (Calendar mysteries) "A Stepping Stone book."
Summary: Bradley, Brian, Nate, and Lucy follow clues on an Easter treasure hunt, while trying to figure out who set it up for them.
ISBN 978-0-375-86116-1 (trade) — ISBN 978-0-375-96116-8 (lib. bdg.)
[1. Mystery and detective stories. 2. Treasure hunt (Game)—Fiction. 3. Easter—Fiction. 4. Twins—Fiction. 5. Brothers and sisters—Fiction. 6. Cousins—Fiction.]
I. Gurney, John Steven, ill. II. Title.
PZ7.R8139Apr 2010 [Fic]—dc22   2009021085

Printed in the United States of America

10 9 8

Contents

1
The Silent Visitor

Bradley Pinto was having a dream. In his dream, he was following a trail of jelly beans. The jelly beans led him into a meadow. The flowers in the meadow were made of lollipops. The trees were sticks of licorice. There was a stream of chocolate milk under whipped-cream clouds. Little butterflies made of cotton candy flew by. One landed on Bradley's ear.

Just as Bradley was about to drink from the chocolate stream, he woke up.

Something *had* touched his ear. Something real!

Bradley opened his eyes in his dark bedroom. He saw a shadowy figure tiptoe toward the door. Then the figure was gone.

Bradley put his hand on his pillow, near his ear. Something was there! It was hard and smooth and sort of round. He turned on his lamp and grabbed the object. It was a plastic Easter egg!

Bradley's twin brother, Brian, sat up and squawked from the next bed, "Hey, what're you doing? It's the middle of the night!"

Bradley looked at the clock. "No it's not," he said. "It's six in the morning the day before Easter!"

"Happy Easter, Bradley," Brian said. Then he went back to sleep.

Bradley sat up and pulled open the two halves of the plastic egg. Inside, he

found a folded note with these words: DON'T WAKE THE GROWN-UPS. SIGNED, THE SHADOW.

"What's going on?" came another voice.

"Morning, Nate," Bradley said, looking down from his bed.

Bradley and Brian's two best friends had slept over. Nate Hathaway and Lucy Armstrong were in sleeping bags on the floor.

Lucy sat up in her sleeping bag. "What time is it?" she asked as she blinked at the light. Lucy's parents were helping build a school on a Native American reservation in Arizona. She was staying with her older cousin, Dink Duncan, while they were gone. Dink was best friends with Nate's big sister, Ruth Rose, and the twins' older brother, Josh. In fact, Dink and Ruth Rose were having a sleepover, too. They were down the hall in Josh's bedroom.

Brian sat up and rubbed his eyes. "Hey, what's this?" he asked. He held up a blue plastic egg. "It was on my pillow!"

"I found one, too," Bradley said, showing his egg. "My egg had a note inside."

Brian yanked his egg apart. A folded paper fell out. "Mine does, too!" he said.

Nate and Lucy soon found plastic eggs on their pillows.

"We all have notes!" Lucy said. "Mine says, GO WHERE A ROSE GROWS. SIGNED, THE SHADOW."

"Mine says, GET DRESSED," Brian said.

Nate crawled out of his sleeping bag. "Mine says, THERE YOU WILL FIND DIRECTIONS TO THE TREASURE. It's signed THE SHADOW, too."

"Cool, it's a treasure hunt!" Lucy said. "I love treasure hunts! But who's the Shadow?"

"Whoever it is, he used a computer," Nate said. "These notes have been printed out."

"Josh has a computer in his room," Brian said.

"Is your brother Josh the Shadow?" Lucy asked.

Brian shrugged. "Maybe. Dink and Ruth Rose slept over last night. I'll bet the three of them cooked up this idea."

"But why put the messages inside Easter eggs?" Nate asked.

"Because tomorrow is Easter, silly!" Bradley said.

"Oh yeah, it is," Nate said. "Happy Easter, guys!"

"I think we should do what the notes say and find the treasure!" Lucy said.

The four kids read their notes again.

"Mine tells us to find the directions," Nate said. "How do we find them?"

"GO WHERE A ROSE GROWS," Lucy said,

reading from her paper. "But where's that?"

"I know!" Nate said. "Over in Center Park there's a rose garden. That's where roses grow!"

Five minutes later, the kids were in the kitchen, pulling on their sneakers.

Lucy saw a basket on the kitchen table. A paper napkin covered something lumpy in the basket. There was a folded paper on top of the napkin. Brian read the note to the other kids:

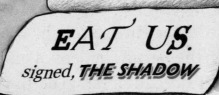

EAT US.

signed, THE SHADOW

Bradley lifted off the napkin. Under it were four jelly doughnuts.

"Yum! I'm beginning to like the Shadow!" Nate said.

2
An Egg Hunt

Bradley found a pencil and wrote another message on the paper. It said:

MOM—WE'RE AT THE PARK. BRADLEY.

The kids hiked down the driveway, toward Center Park. Sunlight was peeking over the barn. The leaves on the tall trees were bright green. The three boys munched on their doughnuts as they walked. Lucy carried the basket holding the fourth doughnut.

"Aren't you gonna eat your doughnut?" Brian asked Lucy. He had finished his and was licking his fingers.

"I'm saving mine for later," Lucy said. "So stop staring at it."

"I wonder what the treasure will be," Nate said.

Bradley laughed. "Knowing Josh, it'll be something to eat."

"But maybe it wasn't Josh who put the notes inside the eggs," Lucy said.

"Then who did?" Brian asked. "Our parents wouldn't do it."

"When I first woke up this morning, I saw someone in our room," Bradley said, "sneaking away from my bed."

"Who was it?" Brian asked.

Bradley shrugged. "It was too dark, and he left the room real fast."

"Did he hop out of the room like a bunny?" Lucy asked. She had a smile on her lips.

Bradley giggled. "No, he glided out like a shadow!" he said.

The kids crossed Pleasant Street and entered Center Park. The rose garden was inside a white picket fence. Most of the rosebushes had small buds on them. Some had early blossoms. The bushes were planted in a big circle around a fountain. A statue of a fish stood on its tail in the fountain. The fish's open mouth spouted water.

On the other side of the rose garden was a pond surrounded by bushes and tall grass. In the middle of the pond was a small island, with a tree in its center.

"Hey, guys, look!" Lucy was pointing at a fat raccoon walking out of some bushes near the pond. Three baby raccoons followed her. They all waddled past the kids and entered a grove of trees.

"They are so cute!" Lucy said.

Just then they heard barking. A man was walking a small white dog through the park. He carried a paper bag in one hand. He stooped over and picked up something from the ground and put it in his bag.

Bradley recognized the man. "Hi, Mr. Pocket!" he called out.

Mr. Pocket waved. "Happy Easter!" he shouted.

"You too!" they all called back.

The kids walked through the gate into the rose garden.

"Well, this is where a rose grows," Bradley said.

"Where do we look?" Brian asked. There were at least a hundred rose-bushes growing in rows. Between the rows was green grass.

"Let's split up," Bradley said. "Each take a row, and check out all the bushes."

"We don't have to do that," Nate said. "Look!" He was pointing at the fountain. A yellow plastic egg floated in the water. He raced toward the fountain with the others right behind him.

Nate got there first. He plucked the egg out of the water.

"Open it!" Brian said.

"It's all wet," Nate said. He wiped the egg on his sweatshirt, then pulled apart the halves.

"There's another note!" Lucy cried.

Nate unfolded the note and read it to the other kids:

THERE ARE ELEVEN MORE PLASTIC EGGS. YOU MUST FIND THE FOUR REAL EGGS TO GET THE TREASURE.

SIGNED, THE SHADOW

Bradley took the note from Nate's fingers. "What does he mean, the *real* eggs?" he asked.

"Real must mean not plastic, like this one," Nate said. He held up the two halves of the one they'd found in the fountain. He put them back together and set the egg in Lucy's basket.

Brian grinned. "Like fried eggs?" he asked. "Gee, I hope the Shadow hid some ketchup. I like ketchup on my eggs!"

Nate laughed out loud. "You crack

me up!" he said. "Get it? *Crack* me up?"

"Let's look for the rest of the eggs," Bradley said.

Center Park covered a wide area. Inside the park were the rose garden, the pond, and a band shell. The band shell was a little platform with a roof over it. In the summertime, musicians played music on the platform. People would gather on the lawn to listen.

A grove of trees grew near the rose garden. Wooden benches had been placed around so people could sit and enjoy the roses.

On one side of the park were the high school playing fields. Next to the high school was a meadow. And next to the meadow was the lawn surrounding Green Lawn Elementary School.

"How do we find Easter eggs in all this?" Brian asked.

"These plastic eggs are bright

colors," Lucy said. "We should be able to see them from far away." She had begun eating her jelly doughnut.

Nate climbed onto one of the benches. He looked around. "I don't see any," he said.

"Let's just start," Bradley said. "We should each look in a different place. I'll go check out the pond."

"I'll search around those trees," Lucy said.

"I'll stay here and look around all the roses," Brian said.

"Okay, I'll snoop around the band shell," Nate said. He wiggled his eyebrows up and down. "Sometimes people drop money there!"

"If you find any, you have to share," Brian said.

"Ha!" Nate said as he raced away.

Carrying her basket, Lucy took off for the grove of trees.

Bradley headed toward the pond. He walked through the tall grass and reeds. He read a sign that said: PLEASE DO NOT FEED THE SWANS.

Bradley stepped carefully up to the water's edge. Last summer, he had seen a long black snake there, lying in the sun. Josh had told him that snapping turtles lived in the pond, too. They came out of the water to lay their eggs.

Bradley placed his feet carefully. He didn't want to step on a snake or a turtle!

At the edge of the pond, Bradley parted a clump of grass. He peered down at the ground. He saw only rocks and mud and weeds, no bright plastic Easter eggs.

Suddenly Bradley froze. He held his breath.

Something was hissing at him!

3
Hissing and Buzzing

Bradley felt goose bumps tickle the hairs on his arms. He stood still, like the fish statue in the fountain. He didn't dare to look down. *Do snapping turtles hiss?* he wondered. Could there be a snake near his feet?

When he didn't hear any more hissing, Bradley looked down. No snapping turtle. No snake that he could see.

Then he noticed something out on the pond. Two swans were floating on the water. They were big and white, with orange bills. The swans watched Bradley. One of them flapped its wide wings and hissed again.

Bradley grinned. He waved at the swans. "Happy Easter, swans!"

The swan kept hissing. The other one let out a loud snort.

"Okay, I'll leave," Bradley said. He stepped away from the pond, watching the ground. Keeping an eye on the swans, he walked all the way around the pond. He saw three caterpillars and a frog, but no eggs. No turtles or snakes, either.

Bradley noticed something dark sticking up from the reeds near the pond. He stepped closer. It was a tree stump that was black and dead.

But on top of the stump was a red plastic Easter egg.

Bradley grabbed the egg. "I found one!" he yelled.

He ran back toward the rose garden with the egg. The other three kids were standing near the fountain.

"We did, too!" Nate said. He and Brian each held a plastic egg.

"Now we have four," Bradley said. He held his egg near his ear and shook it. Something inside it rattled. When Bradley pulled the two halves apart, he found jelly beans. "Just like in my dream!" he said.

"What dream?" Lucy asked.

Bradley told his brother and friends about the candy meadow with chocolate milk in the stream.

"Cool!" Nate said. He found a candy kiss inside the egg he was holding. Brian's egg held a small cookie.

They ate their prizes and put the eggs into Lucy's basket.

"No one has found the real eggs, though," Lucy said.

"Let's keep looking," Bradley said.

They were standing under a tall oak tree. "Maybe if I climb up high, I'll be able to see eggs down on the ground," Lucy said. "Here, hold this."

Lucy handed the basket to Bradley, then started climbing the oak tree. The boys watched her use her hands, feet, and arms as she moved higher.

"She's like a monkey!" Nate said.

"See any eggs?" Bradley called up to Lucy.

"Not yet," she called back. "But I can see our houses!"

Lucy started climbing down. She was on a lower branch when she yelled, "There's one egg up here!"

"Where? Can you get it?" Nate called up to her.

"I think so." Lucy wrapped her legs and one arm around the branch. With her free hand, she reached into a hollow place in the branch. She pulled out a plastic egg. "Here's number five!" she cried.

Bradley held up the basket, and Lucy placed the egg in among the others. Then she swung down to the ground.

"Open it!" Bradley said.

Lucy did, and she found a shiny dime.

"No fair, she gets money!" Brian said.

The others laughed.

"If you'd climbed the tree, you'd have gotten the dime," Lucy said, grinning.

"Okay, what's next?" Nate asked. "We checked the whole park."

"The notes didn't say all the eggs would be in the park," Bradley said. He glanced around. "Maybe some are hidden over by the high school or the elementary school."

"Nate and I will check the high school grounds," Brian said. He and Nate took off running.

"Come on, Lucy," Bradley said. They headed past the band shell toward Silver Circle. They walked onto the lawn that surrounded their school. They both kept their eyes down but saw no eggs in the grass.

"If you were the Shadow, where would you hide the eggs?" Lucy asked Bradley.

Bradley headed toward some playground equipment. "Over there," he said.

They jogged to the swing set. There was also a jungle gym, a seesaw, and a merry-go-round. Bradley put the basket on the ground and sat on a swing. "But I don't see any eggs," he said.

Lucy was on her knees, peering under the merry-go-round. "Well, I do!"

she said. She reached under and pulled out a blue egg.

"Way to go!" Bradley yelled. "That's the sixth egg!"

Lucy opened the egg. "Yum, pink jelly beans!" She offered one to Bradley and ate the other one.

Bradley jumped off the swing and helped Lucy search. They didn't discover any more eggs there.

Then Lucy noticed something. "What's that little house?" she asked.

She was pointing toward a playhouse. It was behind some hedges, next to the school building.

"That's for the kindergarten kids," Bradley said. "They play in it at recess time."

"Let's go check it out," Lucy said.

Bradley grabbed the basket and they ran over. The playhouse had a small door and two windows. There were

flower boxes in front of the windows,
holding plastic flowers.

Lucy crawled inside the playhouse.
"Brad, this is cool!" she said. "Come on
in!"

Bradley got down on his knees and
followed Lucy. Inside, he saw some tiny
furniture. There was a play stove, a little
round table, and four miniature chairs.
Bradley pulled open the stove's oven
door. "Look!" he yelled. A green plastic

egg sat in the oven. "Number seven!"

Bradley found a dime inside the egg. "Ha, my brother is going to be so jealous!" He put the dime in his pocket and the egg in Lucy's basket.

Lucy found egg number eight in one of the window flower boxes. Inside was a small roll of stickers. They searched everywhere else but didn't find any more eggs.

Outside the playhouse, they heard someone yelling. Brian and Nate were running toward them from the high school. They were both shouting and waving their arms.

"Can you hear what they're saying?" Bradley asked Lucy.

"I think Nate is yelling *please*," Lucy said.

"I thought I heard my brother say *knees*," Bradley said.

By then Brian and Nate were almost

at the playhouse. Their faces were red
and their eyes were big.

"BEES!" they both screamed.

4
What's in
Mr. Pocket's Pocket?

"What happened?" Bradley asked.

"Brian poked a bees' nest!" Nate yelled. He and Brian flopped on the ground, out of breath.

"Did you get stung?" Lucy asked.

"No, we ran too fast!" Brian said.

"Did you find any eggs?" Bradley asked.

Nate grinned. "Yeah, we found two on the baseball field," he said. He and Brian each pulled a plastic egg from their pockets. "They were on the pitcher's mound and home plate."

"And they had candy kisses inside," Brian said, rubbing his belly.

"So we've got ten eggs so far," Lucy said. "But we haven't found a real egg yet."

Nate and Brian put their eggs into the basket with the others.

"Where haven't we looked?" Bradley asked.

"How about over there?" Lucy asked. Not far from the playhouse were some wooden farm animals. There were ducks and chickens, cows, sheep, goats, and ponies. The animals had been painted to look real.

The four kids ran over to the make-believe farm. They looked behind the wooden animals and in the grass where they stood.

"Nothing!" Brian said.

"Wait, I see something!" Bradley

yelled. He looked inside a goat's mouth and there was a plastic egg. "This is number eleven!" Bradley found a cookie inside the egg and ate it.

Lucy soon found another egg. It was under the hen, in its make-believe nest. Inside was a tiny plastic mirror.

The kids put the eggs in Lucy's basket. "We have all twelve plastic eggs," she said. "But we still don't have the real ones."

"I don't know where else to look," Bradley said.

"Maybe the eggs hatched," Nate said, "and the little chickens ran away!"

"Talking about eggs is making me hungry," Brian said. "Let's go home and eat breakfast."

The kids hiked up Eagle Lane toward Bradley and Brian's house. The sun over the trees made them squint their eyes.

They clumped up the back steps and

walked into the kitchen. Dink, Josh, and Ruth Rose were there making breakfast. A bowl of pancake batter sat on the counter. Pal sat near Josh's feet, watching him.

"Pancakes, yum, yum!" Brian said. "I'm starving!"

Josh put his finger on his lips. "Shhh, Mom and Dad are still sleeping," he said.

The four kids pulled off their sneakers as quietly as they could.

"Where have you guys been?" Josh went on. He looked upset.

"Searching for these!" Lucy said. She set the egg basket on the table.

"Plastic eggs?" Dink asked. "Where'd you get those?"

"You know where we found them because you hid them," Nate said. "You left notes on our pillows!"

"Notes on your pillows?" Ruth Rose

asked. "What do you mean?"

"Inside plastic eggs!" Lucy added.

"Why would we do that?" Josh asked.

"Because you three are the Shadow!" Bradley cried. He pulled out his note. "This is printed off your computer, Josh!"

Josh laughed. "Okay, we're busted," he said. "We did it. So how many eggs did you find?"

"All of them," Nate said.

Dink, Josh, and Ruth Rose looked in the basket. "I only count twelve," Dink said.

"We couldn't find the four real ones," Lucy said.

"Do we still get the treasure?" Brian asked.

"No way," Josh said. "Wash your hands and let's eat."

The four younger kids washed up,

then pulled chairs to the table.

Soon all seven were gobbling up pan-cakes and drinking juice.

"So where did you hide the real eggs?" Bradley asked.

"Should we tell them?" Josh asked Dink and Ruth Rose.

The other two nodded.

"You know that sign telling people not to feed the swans?" Josh asked.

The four younger kids nodded.

"Well, the real eggs were on the ground, next to the sign," Dink said. "You didn't see them?"

"Nope," Bradley said. "And I would have, because I was standing right next to the sign."

"That's funny," Dink said. "I put them in the grass by the sign."

"Maybe somebody stole them!" Brian said.

Ruth Rose grinned. "The mystery of

the Green Lawn egg thief!" she said.

"How *eggs*-citing!" Josh cracked.

"Anyone want any *eggs*-tra syrup?" Dink asked.

"There was someone else in the park," Lucy said. "That man with the little dog."

"Yeah, Mr. Pocket," Nate said. "I saw him pick up something!"

"I don't think he'd steal Easter eggs from kids," Bradley said.

"But maybe he just saw the eggs and picked them up," Brian said. "What did they look like, Josh?"

"We hard-boiled them, then painted them gold," Josh said.

The seven kids looked at each other.

"Golden eggs," Lucy said. "Anyone would grab one!"

"Hurry up," Bradley said. "I know where Mr. Pocket lives."

5

Raccoon Clues

It took only a few minutes to walk to Indian Way Road, where Mr. Pocket lived. Bradley brought Pal. Pal liked to play with Randolph, Mr. Pocket's dog.

The kids climbed up Mr. Pocket's porch. Bradley rang the bell. They heard barking from inside. A man's voice said, "Hush, Randolph!"

Then Pal barked, too. His big tail swung back and forth.

The door opened, and Mr. Pocket smiled at the kids. "Well, hello," he said.

He was holding a fluffy dog in his arms. "Look, Randolph, we have company!"

Randolph wriggled to get down to play with Pal. Pal tugged on his leash to reach Randolph.

"Hi, Mr. Pocket," Bradley said. "We were wondering if we could ask you some questions."

Mr. Pocket raised his bushy white eyebrows. "Questions about what?" he asked.

"About missing Easter eggs!" Nate said.

"Oooh, a mystery!" Mr. Pocket said. "Come right in!"

The four kids and Pal trooped into Mr. Pocket's living room.

Mr. Pocket set Randolph on the floor. "You can let Pal off his leash," he told Bradley. Bradley did, and the two dogs began to wrestle.

"Please, come in the kitchen," Mr.

Pocket said. "I have something on the stove."

Bradley, Brian, Nate, and Lucy followed Mr. Pocket. He walked over to the stove and stirred something in a pot. "Do you kids like spinach?" he asked.

"No!" shouted Nate and Brian.

"Yes!" shouted Bradley and Lucy.

Mr. Pocket laughed. "Don't worry, I won't make you eat any," he said. "Actually, I'm boiling dandelion greens. They taste even better than spinach."

"You eat dandelions?" Nate asked. "My parents pull them up and throw them away. Aren't dandelions just weeds?"

"Yes, they are weeds," Mr. Pocket said. "But if you pick the leaves before the yellow blossoms open, they make a delicious meal. I just boil them for a few minutes, then add a little butter, salt, and pepper. Yum!"

Mr. Pocket set down his mixing spoon. "Now, what about this egg mystery?" he asked.

The kids told him how Dink, Josh, and Ruth Rose hid some plastic eggs for them to find. "But they also hid four real eggs," Bradley went on. "They painted them gold. They said that if we found

them, we would get a treasure!"

Mr. Pocket smiled. "And did you find the eggs?" he asked.

"No. They told us where they hid the eggs, but they disappeared!" Nate said.

"We remembered seeing you in the park," Lucy added. "We wondered if you saw them."

"No, I only saw the swans and a lot of dandelions," Mr. Pocket said.

Randolph and Pal raced into the kitchen.

"I wonder if Randolph ate the eggs!" Brian said.

Mr. Pocket laughed. "My little dog doesn't like eggs," he said.

"Well, we'd better keep looking," Bradley said. "Thanks a lot, Mr. Pocket. Sorry we disturbed you."

"You didn't disturb me at all," Mr. Pocket said. "Randolph and I love visitors."

He walked the kids to the door. "I hope you solve your mystery," he said.

The four kids walked out onto Mr. Pocket's porch.

"You know, I just thought of something," Mr. Pocket said. He was looking through his screen door. "Raccoons often steal birds' eggs to eat. I saw a family of raccoons this morning. I wonder if they took your eggs."

"We saw them, too," Brian said. "That's a good idea, Mr. Pocket!"

The kids said good-bye, and Bradley put Pal back on his leash. "Let's cut through the park and check one more time," he said.

"Maybe we'll see those raccoons again," Lucy said.

"They'd better not be having eggs for breakfast!" Nate said.

6

Snakes Eat Eggs, Too

"What will we do if the raccoons have the eggs?" Brian asked.

They were waiting for a light to change so they could cross Main Street.

Bradley grinned. "Ask them to give them back," he said.

"What if the eggs are already in their stomachs?" Nate asked.

"Then we'll let them keep them," Bradley said. The kids crossed the street and headed for Center Park.

"I saw the raccoons walk into those

trees," Lucy said. She pointed to the trees near the high school playing fields.

"Maybe they have a home there," Bradley said.

Pal tugged on his leash and led the kids to the trees. He sniffed the ground and whimpered.

"Pal, if I let you off your leash, will you lead us to the raccoons?" Bradley asked the dog.

Pal said, "Woof!"

Bradley unsnapped the leash, and Pal took off, barking. He raced to a tall tree and put his front paws on the trunk.

The kids ran over to the tree. They looked up into the branches. "What does a raccoon nest look like?" Nate asked.

"I think they sleep inside the trunk," Bradley said.

Pal let out another loud bark. He tried to climb the tree.

"Oh my gosh, look!" Lucy said.

About six feet above their heads, a raccoon face peered out of a hole in the tree trunk. The raccoon made a little coughing noise at Pal.

"Now what?" Nate asked, looking up. "We found the nest, but we still don't know if they have our eggs."

"And I'm not climbing up there to look in the nest," Brian added. "Momma Raccoon doesn't look happy to see us."

"I don't think the raccoons took them," Lucy said.

"Why not?" Bradley asked.

"Guys, remember when we saw the raccoons in the park?" Lucy asked. "They walked right past us."

"Yeah, the mom was leading the three babies," Brian said.

"Well, none of them had an egg in its mouth," Lucy said. "And they weren't carrying an egg in their paws, either."

"You're right," Bradley said. "They

were probably just going home to sleep. Raccoons hunt for food at night."

"Maybe they ate the eggs before we saw them," Nate suggested.

"They could have," Bradley said. "But they'd leave the eggshells on the ground. Let's go look!"

The kids ran toward the pond. "Let's split up," Bradley said. "Look everywhere on the ground."

"What if the raccoons ate the eggshells, too?" Brian asked.

Bradley shook his head. "Yuck, I don't think painted eggshells would taste very good!"

The kids walked around the pond. Right away Pal started barking at the swans. They were on the water, flapping their wings.

"Chill out, Mr. and Mrs. Swan," Nate said. "No one is going to hurt you. We're just looking for eggshells."

"Maybe they have a nest some-where," Lucy said. "They think we're going to bother it."

The kids walked quietly and care-fully through the tall grass. Bradley led the way, with Pal in front on his leash. Out on the pond, the two swans kept watch.

"Careful," Bradley whispered over his shoulder. "There may be snakes."

"Who's afraid of snakes?" Brian said.

"I am!" Nate answered.

Suddenly Pal barked and tugged on his leash. Bradley saw the hair on Pal's neck stand up.

"What is it, Pal?" Bradley asked. He looked at the ground in front of Pal.

Then he saw what had made Pal bark. A black snake was curled up in a patch of sunlight.

The snake raised its head and poked its tongue into the air.

Nate came up behind Bradley. "What's going on?" he asked.

Bradley pointed at the snake. "Don't move!" he whispered.

Nate took one look and gasped.

"I couldn't move if I t-tried!" he stammered.

7
Swan Surprise

"What're you guys looking at?" Brian asked. He and Lucy were standing behind Nate.

"S-snake!" Nate said, pointing. "It's a giant, man-eating python!"

"No it isn't," Bradley said. "It's just a big water snake."

"Very big!" Brian said.

"Snakes are shy," Lucy said. "I bet it's more afraid of us than we are of it."

"It couldn't be more afraid than I am!" Nate insisted.

"It's so beautiful," Lucy said. "Look how shiny its scales are."

Pal lowered his nose to sniff the snake. The snake uncurled its long body and started to crawl away.

"What's the matter with its belly?" Brian asked. "It's got a big bump!"

"I think it just ate something," Bradley said.

The kids watched as the snake disappeared in the tall weeds.

"What if it ate one of our eggs?" Nate said. "That bump in its belly looks like an egg!"

"I saw a snake on TV that swallowed an egg whole," Lucy told the boys.

"How do they crack them open?" Brian asked.

"I think their stomach muscles crack the egg once it's inside," Lucy said.

"Oooh, gross!" Nate said.

"Guys, we don't know if that snake

ate our egg," Bradley said. "That lump in its belly could be a frog or something."

"And we don't know if the raccoons did, either," Brian said. "So what do we do?"

"Keep looking for the eggshells," Lucy suggested. "If we find them, at least we'll know something ate our eggs!"

"If we bring the eggshells home, maybe we can still get the prize," Nate said.

When the snake was gone, the kids kept walking.

Pal was still tugging on the leash. His nose was on the ground, sniffing everything.

Suddenly the two swans swam closer to the kids. They began hissing and flapping the water with their wings.

"Guys, I don't think they want us here," Nate said.

"I wonder why," Brian said.

"I know why they're mad at us," Bradley said. "Look." He bent down and parted the grass next to the water's edge. "It's their nest."

The nest was as big around as a tire. It was made of three layers. The bottom layer was twigs and small branches. On top of the branches was a thick layer of grass. The grass was lined with soft swan feathers.

"Oh my goodness!" Lucy said, pointing at the nest.

In the middle of the feathers lay four golden eggs.

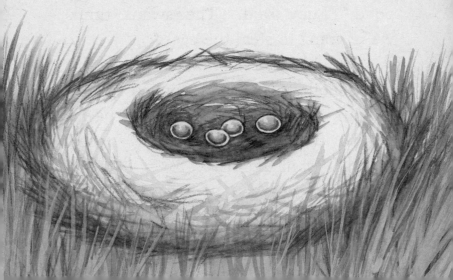

8
Lucy's Brilliant Idea

"We found them!" Nate said. "We get the treasure!"

"Well, the swans really found them first," Bradley said.

"Guys, let's move away from the pond," Lucy said. "The swans think we're going to steal the eggs."

The kids and Pal walked over to the band shell and sat. Pal flopped on the ground with his head on his front paws.

"So what should we do?" asked Brian. "I want the prize!"

"I feel sorry for the swans," Lucy said.

"Why?" asked Nate.

"Because I think something stole their eggs," Lucy said. "Maybe it was the raccoons or that snake. But now they don't have any eggs to hatch. That must be why they took ours."

"Yeah, the swans think the eggs will hatch," Bradley said. "But they won't because they're hard-boiled."

"That's a bummer," Nate said. "The swans will keep waiting and waiting, but nothing will happen."

"I have an idea!" Bradley said. "Let's get them another swan egg. One that will hatch!"

"Where do we get one?" Brian asked.

Bradley stood up and Pal jumped to his feet. "There are swans at the petting zoo," Bradley said. "Maybe they have eggs!"

"Cool!" Nate said. "And we know someone who works there!"

Five minutes later, the kids and Pal walked through the petting zoo gate. They stopped to pet a baby goat. Then they found the office and went inside.

"Well, hi, gang," said a smiling man with gray hair. He was sitting at a desk, typing on a computer. It was Mr. Neater, who used to be the janitor at their school. The kids had helped him find a home for his pet rabbit at the petting zoo.

"Hi, Mr. Neater!" Bradley said. "How's Douglas?"

"Ask him yourself," Mr. Neater said. "He's here, on my lap."

The kids walked closer. A large rabbit was sound asleep on Mr. Neater's knees.

Pal whimpered and tried to lick Douglas. Bradley held the leash tightly.

"Can I pet him?" Lucy asked.

Mr. Neater smiled. "Douglas will be sad if you don't!" he said.

Lucy patted the rabbit's soft head. Douglas twitched his ears and wiggled his tail.

"What brings you kids here?" Mr. Neater asked.

Bradley told Mr. Neater about the

golden eggs in the swans' nest.

"My goodness, that is a problem," Mr. Neater said. "It's a sad thing, but a lot of wild birds lose their eggs to other animals who want to eat them."

"We were wondering if the petting zoo still has swans," Bradley said.

"Why, yes, we have a pair out in the barn," Mr. Neater said. Then he grinned. "Say, I'll bet I know what you're thinking. You want one of their eggs, right?"

"Do they have any eggs, Mr. Neater?" Nate asked.

Mr. Neater nodded. "You bet. I think they have a bunch this season."

"Wow! Could we get one?" Bradley asked.

"Let's go talk to Tom, our swan expert," Mr. Neater said. He put Douglas on the floor and stood up. "Follow me!"

Mr. Neater led the kids and Pal into

a small barn. The first thing they saw was a mother hen and a batch of yellow baby chicks.

"Over this way," Mr. Neater said. They followed him to a pen. Inside the pen, two swans were lying on some straw. An open door led to an outdoor area with a small pond. "The momma is the one with her head down. And there is her clutch of eggs."

Bradley gasped. Up close, the swans were really big! They were as white as snow, with orange beaks and bright, shiny eyes.

"Hi, Mr. Neater," a voice said. A young man walked over to the pen. He was wearing a dark green sweatshirt with a PETTING ZOO patch on one sleeve.

"Hi, Tom," Mr. Neater said. He introduced the kids and Pal. Then he told Tom about the swans in the park.

"My young friends here are hoping

your swans won't mind giving one of their eggs," Mr. Neater said.

"I'm sure they won't mind," Tom said. "In fact, they have too many eggs. They usually lay from three to eight, but this year we have ten!"

Tom entered the pen and spoke softly to the mother swan. Then he reached into the nest and pulled out two greenish-colored eggs. "These should hatch in about ten days," Tom said. "But we have to put them in the new nest pretty fast."

"But what if the snake or raccoons eat them before they hatch?" Bradley asked.

Tom put the eggs inside his sweat-shirt pocket. "That's always a problem,"

he said. He looked at Mr. Neater. "Any suggestions?"

The man shook his head.

"I have an idea!" Lucy said.

They all listened as she explained.

"You know, that just might work," Tom said. "I'll meet you guys out front in five minutes!"

9
Happy Swans, Hungry Kids

While they waited, the kids played with the baby goat. He nibbled on their fingers and licked the palms of their hands.

"Okay, we're all set!" Tom said a few minutes later. He came back with a tall man wearing a green sweatshirt like his. "This is Luke. He's a volunteer like Mr. Neater, and he's going to help us."

Luke was carrying a plastic kiddie pool. "We use this for ducklings," he said. "But it'll be perfect for your project."

The three adults, four kids, and Pal

headed back to Center Park.

"Can you take us to the swans' nest?" Tom asked.

"Sure," Bradley said. He and Pal led the way.

"Look," Lucy whispered as they approached the nest.

One of the swans was lying on the nest. The other one swam in the pond nearby.

"The mother is on the nest," Luke whispered. "Her mate keeps an eye on her to make sure she's safe."

"That poor mother swan is trying to hatch the eggs," Mr. Neater said.

"Okay, to make this work, we need to get her off the nest," Luke said. He walked toward the nest, waving the kiddie pool.

The mother swan hissed at him, but she hopped off her nest and backed away. Never taking her eyes off the humans, she waded into the pond. She joined her mate and glared at the intruders.

With the mother swan out of the nest, everyone could see the golden Easter eggs.

Mr. Neater removed the eggs and handed them to the four kids.

Suddenly the mother swan streaked over toward the kids, hissing and snapping her beak. Luke and Tom waved their arms, and she went back to the pond. But she did not look happy.

"It's okay, Momma Swan," Mr. Neater said. "Pretty soon, you'll have babies to keep you busy!"

"Ready to get wet?" Tom asked Luke and Mr. Neater. He kicked off his sneakers.

"How deep is the water?" Mr. Neater asked. He was pulling off his shoes and socks.

"Not very," Luke said, removing his sneakers. "I helped clean up some litter last year. I only got wet up to my knees."

"Can we help?" Bradley asked.

"Absolutely," Tom said. "After all, this was your idea! But first, this."

Very gently, Tom took the two real swan eggs out of his sweatshirt pouch. He laid them in the center of the swans' nest.

"Now let's gather around the nest," Tom said. "All seven of us will lift it together and place it inside the kiddie pool."

"Careful not to let the nest break apart," Mr. Neater said.

On a count of three, they picked up the nest and set it into the plastic pool.

"Great!" Tom said. "Now Mr. Neater, Luke, and I will float it out to the island. I think the water is too deep for you kids."

The three adults waded into the water. They floated the kiddie pool—with the swan nest inside—between them. The two swans hissed and flapped their wings. They followed the group to the island.

Bradley, Brian, Lucy, and Nate watched them lift the nest out and set it on the island rocks. Then the three adults came back with the kiddie pool.

"This should be interesting," Tom said. He sat on the shore. "Let's watch and see what they do."

The two swans swam up to the little island. They stretched their long necks and looked inside their nest. Then they both began grunting.

"They've seen the eggs!" Bradley said.

It took just a few seconds for the mother swan to sit on the eggs. Her mate stayed near the nest.

"I think the problem has been solved," Mr. Neater said. He grinned at the kids. "That was a great idea!"

"So now the raccoons and snakes won't be able to get their eggs, right?" Nate said.

"That's right," Tom said. "Where the nest was before, any creature could sneak up and steal the eggs while Momma Swan was off the nest. But now, if a raccoon or snake swims to the island, the swans would see it coming and fight it off."

"And trust me," Luke said, "swans are excellent fighters!"

They all sat on the bank and watched the swans for a while.

"I can't wait to see the babies," Lucy said.

"Come back in about two weeks," Tom said. "Baby swans are called cygnets, and they're real cute!"

After a while, Bradley stood up. "Well, we have our golden eggs," he said. "Let's go home and get our treasure!"

The kids thanked Mr. Neater, Tom, and Luke. Then they headed across the park toward Bradley and Brian's house.

Five minutes later, the four kids and Pal burst into the kitchen. Dink, Josh, and Ruth Rose were at the table, playing Monopoly.

"We got them!" Bradley announced.

They each placed one golden egg on the table.

"Yeah, now we want the treasure!" Nate said. "And I hope it's not Monopoly money!"

"It's not money at all," Josh said. He walked over to the refrigerator.

"See, I told you, it's food!" Bradley said.

"Good, because I'm starving!" Brian said.

Josh opened the fridge and pulled out four tall chocolate Easter bunnies.

"Awesome!" Nate said. Right away he broke off a chocolate ear and began chewing.

"So, where did you guys find the golden eggs?" Dink asked.

"It's a long story," Bradley said.

Dink, Josh, and Ruth Rose just looked at him.

"So, we're waiting!" Ruth Rose said.

"We fought off a giant snake!" Nate said.

"And a pack of hungry raccoons!" Brian added.

"And we had to swim in the pond!" Lucy put in.

The three older kids stared.

"Is this all true?" Josh asked.

Bradley licked his chocolate bunny. "Of course it's true," he said. "Would we tell a lie the day before Easter?"

If you like Calendar Mysteries,
you might want to read
A to Z Mysteries!

Help Dink, Josh, and Ruth Rose . . .

. . . solve mysteries from A to Z!

Track down all these books
for a little mystery in your life!

A to Z Mysteries®
by Ron Roy

Calendar Mysteries
by Ron Roy

Capital Mysteries
by Ron Roy

Marion Dane Bauer
The Blue Ghost
The Green Ghost
The Red Ghost
The Secret of the Painted House

Polly Berrien Berends
The Case of the Elevator Duck

Éric Sanvoisin
The Ink Drinker

George Edward Stanley
Ghost Horse

How many of KC and Marshall's adventures have you read?

Capital Mysteries

- [ ] #1 Who Cloned the President?
- [ ] #2 Kidnapped at the Capital
- [ ] #3 The Skeleton in the Smithsonian
- [ ] #4 A Spy in the White House
- [ ] #5 Who Broke Lincoln's Thumb?
- [ ] #6 Fireworks at the FBI
- [ ] #7 Trouble at the Treasury
- [ ] #8 Mystery at the Washington Monument
- [ ] #9 A Thief at the National Zoo
- [ ] #10 The Election-Day Disaster
- [ ] #11 The Secret at Jefferson's Mansion